To order additional copies of this book, contact:
Xlibris
844-714-8691
www.Xlibris.com
Orders@Xlibris.com

ISBN: Softcover   978-1-6641-4400-2
        Hardcover   978-1-6641-4401-9
        EBook   978-1-6641-4399-9

Print information available on the last page

Rev. date: 03/05/2021

Dedications

To my children for their continuous support.

Thank you to my grandchildren who, unbeknownst to them, were contributors to this book.

To all the people who think all Grammys say, "yes," you were the inspiration for this book! ☺

Thank you to my husband who is my sounding board, my technology expert, and my constant supporter.

Thank you to Cheryl who took the time out of her busy life to be one of my very first readers, giving me much encouragement.

And, of course, I thank God for continuing to inspire & encourage me down this path of writing books in order to help children in some way.

Grammy said, "NO! You can't put pickles, chocolate, pretzels, olives, chips, cheese, and raisins in a peanut butter sandwich!"

And then Grammy thought, *Why not?*

"Mmmmm, this is good!" said Grammy.

Grammy said, "NO! You can't go outside to play because it's raining!"

And then Grammy said, "Why not?"

"This is fun!" said Grammy.

Grammy said, "NO! You can't build a bike ramp!"

And then Grammy said, "Why not?"

"Wheeeee!" said Grammy.

Grammy said, "NO! You can't paint the swing set six different colors!"

And then Grammy said, "Why not?"

"This is going to look so pretty," said Grammy.

And then one day, Grammy said,
"NO! You shouldn't climb so high up
in that tree. It's not safe."

And then Grammy said, "This one's much safer. And we can have a snack!"

Grammy said, "NO! You can't go swimming until I go out there with you. You should never swim without an adult watching you."

And then Grammy said, "Now we're ready! Let's have fun!"

Grammy does say "NO" sometimes because she loves us.

But we know Grammy will always
say "YES" to ice cream!

"This is the swing set that my grandsons painted with my husband and I. The color scheme was their creation!"

The US Review of Books

"You can't put pickles, chocolate, pretzels, olives, chips, cheese, and raisins in a peanut butter sandwich!"

Sometimes there are reasons Grandma has to say "no," such as in matters of safety. Other times, when the initial answer is "no," Grammy then reconsiders. "Why not?" she thinks to herself. No harm will be done, and it might even be fun. In this delightful children's picture book, that's precisely what happens in a series of events, including the creative culinary decision to embellish a basic peanut butter sandwich with such outlandish ingredients as olives and raisins. The little boy and girl laugh, realizing it is quite delicious as they eat with Grammy.

Playing outside in the rain at first elicits a "no" from Grammy, but after her thinking, "Why not?" the three again enjoy silly fun. And when the children want to paint the swing set six different colors, Grammy says "no," but then reconsiders, declaring, "This is going to look so pretty." However, Grammy is quite firm in her "no" when it comes to the children going swimming without her, explaining they must never swim without an adult present. And so the three enjoy the pool together.

Geddes' fun and brightly illustrated book is a fantastic selection to read with any group of small children. One can imagine the kids saying together in chorus, "Grammy says, 'No!'" The important lesson imparted is that while sometimes it is okay to do silly things—with the permission of a parent or grandparent—there are other times when the answer must be "no." These would include any situations involving their safety, health, and wellbeing. But no doubt about it, Grammy finds creative and slightly unusual ways to have fun with her grandbabies. Featured at the book's end is a photograph of Geddes with the motley-colored swing set her real-life grandchildren painted, for which they developed the decorative color scheme.

CPSIA information can be obtained
at www.ICGtesting.com
Printed in the USA
BVHW060131070421
604335BV00014B/376